What will
you dream
of tonight?

For Annie. Dream up your dreams – F. S. xx
For Jack – A. A.

First published 2019 by Nosy Crow Ltd, The Crow's Nest
14 Baden Place, Crosby Row, London SE1 1YW
www.nosycrow.com

ISBN 978 1 78800 493 0 (HB)
ISBN 978 1 78800 545 6 (PB)

Nosy Crow and associated logos are trademarks
and/or registered trademarks of Nosy Crow Ltd.

Text © Frances Stickley 2019
Illustrations © Anuska Allepuz 2019

A CIP catalogue record for this book is available from the British Library.

Printed in China
Papers used by Nosy Crow are made from wood grown in sustainable forests.

1 3 5 7 9 8 6 4 2 (HB)
1 3 5 7 9 8 6 4 2 (PB)

nosy crow

Frances Stickley & Anuska Allepuz

What will you dream of tonight?

Tucked into bed with a world in your head
as we cuddle and turn down the light.
Where will you go when the stars start to glow?
Tell me, what will you dream of tonight?

Drifting away at the end of the day
as the spellbinding sun disappears.
What will you choose?
You have nothing to lose . . .

. . . because anything's possible here!

So, float through the sky like a soft lullaby,
carried over the rivers and streams,
and soar to the moon in a midnight balloon.
You can go anywhere in your dreams.

Will you be brave on the crest of a wave
as you cruise through the sea to the light?
How far will you sail on the tail of a whale?
Will you dream of the ocean tonight?

Sandcastles stand on the beach where you land
as the waves crash and curl with the tide.
But listen, there's more . . .
. . . there's a shipwreck on shore.
Will you dare to explore what's inside?

Maybe you'll fly through the dark endless sky
as the asteroids race with your rocket.
Maybe you'll land with a star in your hand
that you'll keep, safe and sound, in your pocket.

You might take a ride down a waterfall slide
as you glide through a tropical sky
and swing past the leaves on a jungle trapeze.
You are free! You are fast! You can fly!

Or what if you go where the stars meet the snow
and the Arctic lights shimmer and spark,
then follow a track on a polar bear's back
as the night rainbows dance in the dark?

Flying again over dark desert plains
as the night lanterns flicker and fade,
you sail and you swoop in a smooth loop-the-loop
through a magical midnight parade.

Will you feel scared as you enter the lair
where a treasure chest gleams in the light?
If you tiptoe and creep, he just might stay asleep.
Will you dream of the dragon tonight?

Or maybe you'll dream that you're floating downstream
through a woodland of whispering trees,
where nightingales nest as the forest folk rest
on a beautiful blanket of leaves.

Now, cuddle up tight and we'll whisper goodnight
as we drift into darkening skies.
And I promise I'll stay just a heartbeat away.
I'll be here when you open your eyes.

So, tucked into bed, with a world in your head
and a ceiling of stars up above,
wherever you go, I just want you to know . . .

. . . you are safe.
You are lovely.
You're loved.